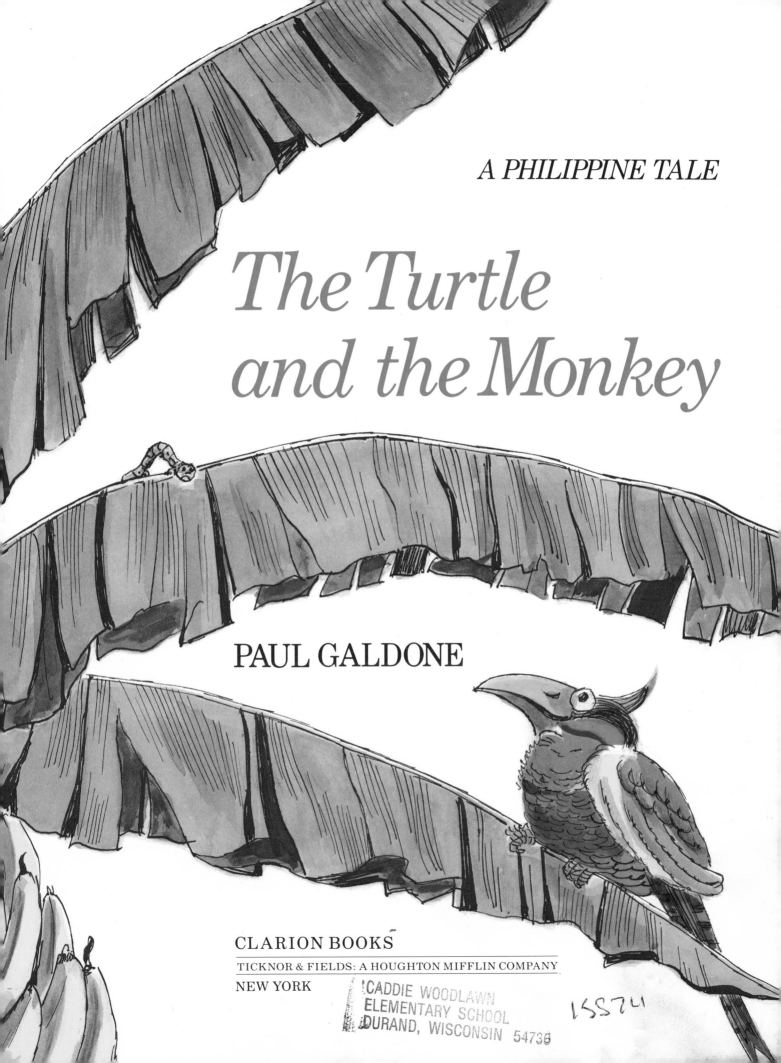

A PHILIPPINE TALE

The Turtle and the Monkey

PAUL GALDONE

CLARION BOOKS

TICKNOR & FIELDS: A HOUGHTON MIFFLIN COMPANY

NEW YORK

For Gloria and Jack

Clarion Books
Ticknor & Fields, a Houghton Mifflin Company
Copyright © 1983 by Paul Galdone
Printed in the U.S.A.

Library of Congress Cataloging in Publication Data
Galdone, Paul.
The turtle and the monkey.

Summary: In order to get her share of the
banana tree she has found floating in the river,
Turtle must outwit the very greedy Monkey.
[1. Animals—Fiction.   2. Banana—Fiction]
I. Title.
PZ7.G1305Tu   1983   [E]   82-9596
ISBN 0-89919-145-2

H 10 9 8 7 6 5 4 3 2 1

One day, as Turtle was sunning herself, she saw something floating down the river. "Why, it's a banana tree!" she said.

She dove into the river, swam to the tree and pulled it to shore.

But try as she might, she couldn't get it
up onto high ground.

Turtle went and found Monkey and brought him back to see the tree.

"I saved this banana tree from the river," she told him. "Help me carry it to my garden, and I will plant it."

"If I help you, I should get a share of the tree," said Monkey, who loved bananas more than anything.

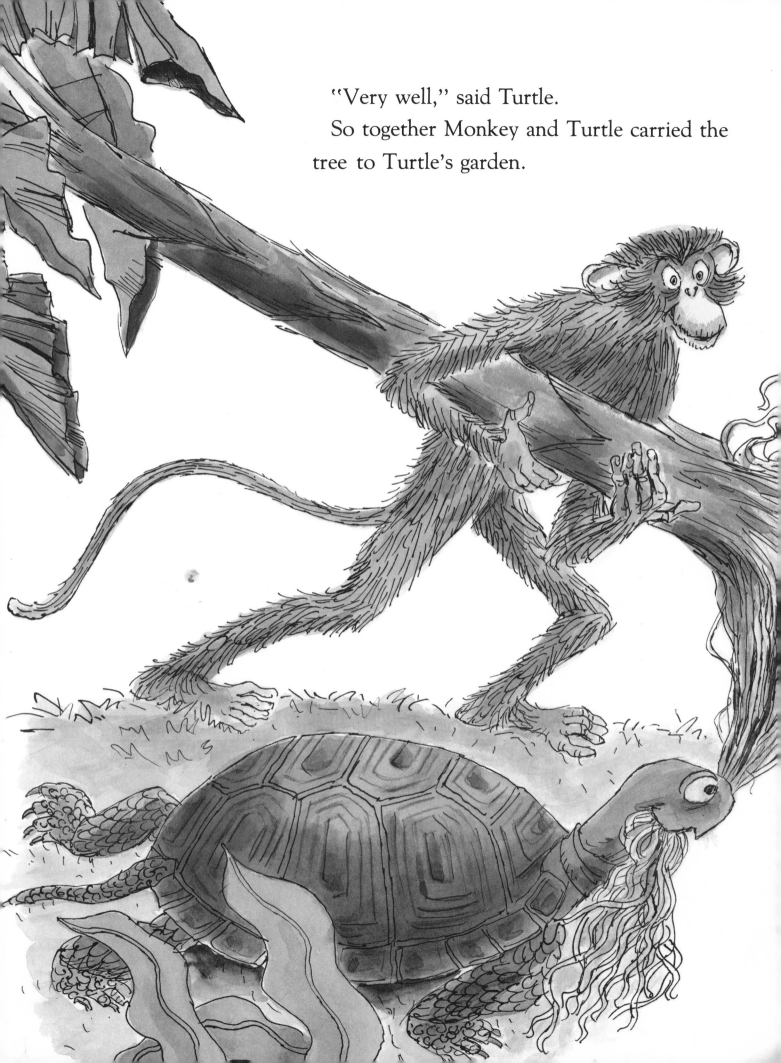

"Very well," said Turtle.
So together Monkey and Turtle carried the
tree to Turtle's garden.

"Now we have to dig a hole for the tree," said Turtle.
"Oh, no," said Monkey. "We agreed we would share it."
"So we did," replied Turtle. "But first we have to plant it.
Then, when it grows bananas, we'll each take half."

"That's no way to share," said Monkey. "We must each take half of the tree now."

"But that's not a good way to share a tree," said Turtle.

"I don't care," yelled Monkey. "I want my share now!"

Slowly, Turtle cut the tree in half.
Monkey looked at the two halves.
With its big green leaves, the top half
seemed to be the best.

So Monkey grabbed it and said,
"This top part is mine."

Then he put it over his shoulder and
hurried off to his garden to plant it.

Turtle looked at the stem that was left.
She dug a hole, and carefully planted the stem.
Then she brought water from the river and
wet the earth around it.

Under the hot sun
Monkey's half of the tree,
which had no roots,
soon wilted and died.

But Turtle's half grew strong and tall
and soon new leaves appeared.
By and by bananas began growing
near the top.

When the bananas were ripe Turtle wanted to
pick them, but she couldn't climb the tree.

Once again she brought Monkey to her garden.
"If you climb the tree and throw down the bananas,
I will give you some of them," she said.

In no time Monkey
reached the top of the tree.
He decided to sample the bananas.
Turtle waited, but Monkey didn't
throw down any bananas.

Instead he ate one after another!

"Throw me some bananas," called Turtle.

"No, I won't," said Monkey. "You cheated me by giving me the half of the tree that wouldn't grow. Now I'm going to eat my fill!"

"Just throw me a few," called Turtle.

"Here, have some skins," called Monkey.
And he threw down a handful.

Now that made Turtle mad!
She went and gathered thorns and
prickers and put them all around the tree.

Then she hid in the bushes.

After Monkey had eaten all the bananas he wanted, he jumped down from the tree.

"E-e-e-e-e!" he shrieked as he stepped on the thorns and prickers.

Turtle couldn't help laughing when she saw Monkey hopping about.

Monkey heard Turtle laughing and pulled her out of her hiding place. Then he turned her on her back.

Helplessly she kicked her legs in the air.

"Now I'm going to punish you!" said Monkey. "How would you like me to do it? Should I dig a deep hole and put you in it? Or should I tie you to your banana tree? Or should I take you to the top of the tallest mountain and leave you there?"

Turtle thought quickly and then said: "I wouldn't mind if you left me on a tall mountain, or tied me to my banana tree, or even if you dropped me in a deep hole. You can do whatever you want with me, but please, oh please, don't throw me into the water!"

Monkey was overjoyed when he heard this. "Since water is what you fear most, that will be your punishment!"

He picked up Turtle,
carried her to the river,

and threw her way out into the middle
where the water was deepest.

There was a great splash, then Turtle sank out of sight.
Monkey danced with glee. He was sure he would
never see Turtle again. But just then . . .

. . . Turtle's head popped to the surface. "Thank you, Friend Monkey," she said. "You didn't know the water is my real home, did you?"

And then she paddled happily downstream.